This edition published by Parragon in 2012
Parragon
Queen Street House
4 Queen Street
Bath BA1 1HE, UK
www.parragon.com

Edited by: Katrina Hanford   Designed by: Jim Willmott
Production by: Joanne Knowlson

ISBN 978-1-4454-6482-4

Printed in China

Bath • New York • Singapore • Hong Kong • Cologne • Delhi
Melbourne • Amsterdam • Johannesburg • Auckland • Shenzhen

Down in the deepest ocean, there once lived a mermaid princess called Ariel. She was the youngest daughter of King Triton, ruler of the merpeople, and she had the most beautiful singing voice in the whole of his kingdom.

Her father loved her dearly, but she was always getting into trouble.

Ariel longed to be part of the human world and spent her time exploring old shipwrecks.

When Ariel was sixteen years old, King Triton arranged for her to sing in a magnificent concert, and merpeople came from all over the kingdom to hear her.

That evening Ariel was so busy exploring with her friend Flounder that she forgot all about the concert! She had found some human treasures and taken them to the surface to ask Scuttle the seagull what they were.

The Sea-King feared for her safety and, thinking
humans were dangerous, warned her to stay away from
them. But the little mermaid was certain he was wrong.
King Triton was furious. "You could have been seen by one
of those humans!" he raged. "I'm never to hear of you going
to the surface again. Is that clear?" Ariel tried to protest but
her father wouldn't listen.

He ordered Sebastian, Ariel's music teacher, to keep an eye on her. But it wasn't an easy task!

One day Sebastian followed Ariel and Flounder to the surface to watch a ship!

On board the crew were celebrating the birthday of a handsome prince called Eric, and Ariel watched them in delight.

Soon storm clouds gathered overhead. Huge waves
wrecked the ship and Eric was flung into the sea. Ariel swam
quickly to his rescue and pulled him towards the shore.

"Look! He's breathing!" cried Ariel. She gazed at Eric and fell deeply in love. Then, as she sang to him, his eyes began to open. But, hearing a voice in the distance, Ariel slipped back into the water and hid behind a nearby rock. She watched as Eric's servant led him away.

When they were out of sight, Ariel swam home. "Some day," she vowed to herself, "I'm going to be part of that human world."

Sebastian had seen everything, and it was not long before the Sea-King learnt that Ariel was in love with a human. Triton was very angry. Determined to teach his daughter a lesson, he stormed into her secret grotto and destroyed all her beloved human treasures.

Heartbroken, Ariel sat down and wept. Above her, two sly-looking eels called Flotsam and Jetsam emerged from the shadows. The little mermaid looked up.

"Poor sweet child," they hissed. "Don't be scared. We know someone who can make all your dreams come true. Ursula has great powers."

"The Sea-Witch!" gasped Ariel. She knew that Ursula was her father's worst enemy, who had been banished from his kingdom many years ago and who was now seeking revenge. Ariel hesitated. Then, thinking that it was her only chance to win Prince Eric's love, the little mermaid swam away with the evil eels – quickly followed by Flounder and Sebastian.

Ursula greeted Ariel gleefully. "The only way to get what you want," the Sea-Witch explained, "is to become human yourself. And fortunately I know a little magic."

"Now listen, here's the deal. In exchange for your voice, I will turn you into a human for three days. If Eric hasn't given you the kiss of true love in that time, you will become a mermaid again and belong to me for ever." A scroll appeared in Ursula's hand. "Go ahead and sign," she urged.

Ariel was terrified but, thinking of Eric again, she signed.

A moment later she was walking on the seashore – a human at last.

Prince Eric had been searching everywhere for the girl with the beautiful voice who had rescued him. He had almost given up hope of finding her, when he noticed someone sitting on a rock. This girl looked familiar but, when he found she couldn't speak, Eric realized sadly that she wasn't the one. Feeling sorry for the voiceless girl, he led her back to the palace. And the next day, Eric took Ariel on a tour of his kingdom. They enjoyed being together and Ariel was sure the prince was falling in love with her.

Later that afternoon, when they were boating on a lake, Eric bent forward to kiss Ariel – but at that very moment the boat was overturned.

The Sea-Witch had been watching them and, fearing her plan was about to fail, she sent her precious eels to take action.

Later, disguised as Vanessa, a beautiful maiden –
with Ariel's voice trapped in a seashell necklace, Ursula
made her way to the shore, where she captured Prince
Eric under her spell.

Eric led Vanessa to the palace, and the very next day announced that they were to be married. The wedding ship was to depart at sunset.

Ariel and her friends watched in despair as the sun lowered in the sky.

By chance, Scuttle discovered that Vanessa was
really Ursula in disguise, and he called on all the
sea creatures to stop the wedding. Sebastian went to
find the Sea-King and Flounder helped Ariel towards
the wedding ship.

Suddenly birds swooped down on Vanessa.
A lobster pinched her nose and some seals flipped
her into the wedding cake! In the chaos, Vanessa's
seashell necklace broke and the beautiful voice
inside flew back to its rightful owner.

Eric, released from the spell, took Ariel in his arms. Just as he was about to kiss her, the sun sank below the horizon. Straightaway Ariel was turned back into a mermaid. Ursula grabbed her and dived into the water. Her evil cackle echoed eerily around the ship.

"Ursula, stop!" thundered King Triton, rearing up in front of the Sea-Witch. "Let her go!"

"No!" cried Ursula. "She's mine now. You see, we made a deal! However, I might be willing to make an exchange for someone even better," she suggested slyly.

Triton felt he had no choice. He changed the signature on the scroll to his own and handed over his magic trident to the Sea-Witch.

"At last! It's all mine." Ursula screamed. "I am the ruler of the ocean!" Just then a sharp pain shot through her arm. It was a harpoon thrown by Eric. He had come to rescue Ariel.

The Sea-Witch swelled with anger and towered above them. She summoned all the sea's power and stirred up a giant whirlpool, dragging up ancient shipwrecks from the seabed.

Eric scrambled on board one of the decks and, somehow, he reached the ship's steering wheel. Using all his might he aimed the broken bow directly at Ursula. And with a terrible scream she disappeared under the sea.

Triton's power was instantly restored. He rose to the surface and saw Ariel gazing lovingly at Eric, who was lying on the beach.

"She really does love him," Triton murmured to Sebastian. "I suppose the only problem left is how much I will miss her." Then, with a flourish of his trident, the Sea-King granted Ariel her dearest wish – to be human forever. Overjoyed, Eric and Ariel rushed into each other's arms.

   A few days later the couple were married, and all their
friends were invited to the wedding. King Triton gladly gave
Ariel and Eric his blessing, knowing they would live happily
ever after.